Tweenies™

Jump, Doodles, Jump

The Tweenies were in the garden, playing with Jake's bouncy ball.
It was very hard to catch. Just then, Izzles raced into the garden,
jumped up and caught the ball in her mouth.

"WOWEE!" cried Jake. "What a jumper!"

"Let's see if Izzles can jump over my arm," said Fizz. "Come on Izzles, JUMP!"

Izzles crouched down, wagged her tail...and leapt right over Fizz's arm.

"Clever Izzles," cooed the Tweenies. "The best jumper in the world."

Doodles was watching from under the slide.

"Have a go, mate," said Milo, and held out his arm.

Doodles rushed towards Milo, skidded straight under

his arm and landed in the flower bed.

"Oh, Doodles, you are funny," laughed Jake.

"You're no good at jumping," Milo told him.

"You'd better leave it to Izzles," added Bella.

Poor Doodles! He picked himself up, padded indoors to his beanbag and hid his head in shame.

Fizz followed Doodles into the playroom.
"Doodles, don't be upset," she told him.
"I'm sure you could be good at jumping."
"It's no good," Doodles muttered.
"I want to jump but I just can't."

"Let's ask the computer about
jumping," Fizz suggested. She
switched it on and pointed
at the screen. "These are all
really good jumpers."

"A frog,

a kangaroo

and a
tiny little
grasshopper."

"But how do they do it?" Doodles asked.

"I'll pretend to be them, and then you can ask me," Fizz replied.

"Oh, all right," Doodles sighed.

"Look," said Fizz. "I'm a grasshopper.
Ask me how I jump."

"Hey, little grasshopper," sang Doodles,
"how do you do?

Can you teach me how to jump just like you?"

"OK," squeaked Fizz in a grasshopper voice. "This is what I do."

Fizz crouched down. Then she leapt
into the air and landed beside Doodles.
"Your turn," she said. "Jump, Doodles, jump."
Doodles crouched down just like
Fizz but, instead of springing into
the air, he fell forwards and
landed on his nose.

"Never mind," Fizz told him. "Maybe a frog is easier."

"Hey, Mr Froggy," Doodles sang,
"how do you do?
Can you teach me how to jump
just like you?"
"Watch me," croaked Fizz.

Then she leapt across the
room in long, froggy jumps.
"Your turn," she said.
"Jump, Doodles, jump."

Doodles tried his hardest to copy Fizz but, instead of long, froggy jumps, he fell head over heels.

"Poor Doodles," said Fizz. "Let's try the kangaroo."

"Mrs Kangaroo," sang Doodles,
"how do you do?
Can you teach me how to jump
just like you?"

"Boing, boing, boing!"
cried Fizz as she bounced round
the room like a kangaroo.

Doodles watched Fizz carefully.

"Your turn," she said.

"Jump, Doodles, jump."

"Boing!" he barked, "boing!"

He bent his knees, jumped

towards Fizz...and

knocked her over.

"Be careful, Doodles," Fizz complained.

"But I jumped," Doodles said happily.

"Let's go and show the others."

Fizz and Doodles went into the garden.

"Listen, everybody!" shouted Fizz.

"Doodles has something to show you."

"I can JUMP!" Doodles said.

"Oh, Doodles," said Bella. "You tried that before."

"But we've been practising," said Fizz. "Watch!"

Fizz put a big soft block in the middle of the garden.

"Now, Doodles," she told him, "jump right over it.

Remember, you're a kangaroo. Boing!"

"Boing!" Doodles repeated. Then he bent his knees, jumped...

...and landed right on top of the block.
The Tweenies laughed and laughed.

"Never mind, Doodles," they told him. "We can play jumping
with Izzles instead. She's really good at it."

Doodles plodded back indoors.

"Izzles can jump but I can't," he said, sadly. "No one wants a dog that can't jump. I'll just have to pack my bag and leave."

Doodles started packing his favourite things into his doggy bag, but then he began to yawn.

"I'll just have a little sleep before I go. Oh, how I wish I could jump."

While Doodles was asleep, he dreamt he was Doodles the Wonderdog, taking part in a dog jumping competition.

That was a fab-a-rooney jump. And now Doodles the Wonderdog is going to attempt the high jump at three metres. That's very high!

Ooooh!

Ooooh!

BOING!

He's over! Another meg-a-rooney jump!
Doodles the Wonderdog has won the gold medal!

Here you are,
Doodles the
Wonderdog.

Thank you.

Doodles woke up.

"Oh dear," he said. "It was only a dream.
I still can't jump. I'll be on my way."

So he picked up his doggy bag and headed
for the front door.

The Tweenies and Izzles were coming in from the garden when they saw Doodles with his doggy bag. Izzles bounded up to Doodles and looked at him anxiously.

"Oh, Doodles, you're not leaving home, are you?" Bella asked. Doodles nodded.

"But why?" asked Fizz.

"Because I can't *jump*," said Doodles. "No one wants a dog that can't *jump*."

"We don't mind," said the Tweenies. "You're clever and cuddly and the best listener in all the world."

"And we love you," Jake added.

"Really?" asked Doodles. Then his tail began to wag, his eyes sparkled and, with a loud **"BOING!"**...

...Doodles jumped for joy!

THE END